The Town That Forgot about Christmas

by Susan K. Leigh

Adapted from *The City That Forgot about Christmas*
by Mary Warren

ILLUSTRATED BY DAVID GORDON

CONCORDIA PUBLISHING HOUSE · SAINT LOUIS

Not so very long ago

and not so very far away,

a sad thing happened in a busy little town.

The people who lived there had grown selfish and wicked. Children shouted and fought. They didn't play together. They didn't share. Grown-ups scowled and complained. They didn't help each other. They didn't care.

Everyone was rude and cranky and mean.

The saddest thing of all was that the people in this town had forgotten the meaning of Christmas. They had forgotten about Jesus, the Son of God.

For these people, Christmas Day was like any other day. No one sang joyous Christmas songs. No mothers cooked a special Christmas dinner. No fathers helped their children trim a Christmas tree. There were no pretty packages and no nativity sets and no twinkling lights.

Can you imagine it? No Christmas?

One day an unusual man from a far away place came to this town. His name was Matthew.

Matthew was surprised and dismayed when he learned the people had forgotten Christmas. "What?" he cried. "Not one of you remembers the message of the angels? Well, well, well," Matthew said to no one in particular. "We shall see about that."

Now Matthew was a kind man and a merry one.

He had worked his whole life as a carpenter and knew how to make many things out of wood. Matthew could build big things and little things. And he could carve the wood as well. He could make tops and whistles, dolls and jumping jacks, carts and building blocks.

As the children in the busy town came to know Matthew, they would trail after him just to see what he would make next.

As time went on, the women of the town learned that Matthew was good at fixing things. "Here comes Matthew," one would call to another. "Perhaps he will mend my cabinet door." "When Matthew comes," someone else would say, "I shall ask him to make a window box for my pansies."

All the men of the town liked having Matthew around too. Matthew helped them fix things and he taught them to work with wood.

With Matthew's encouragement, the parents started playing games with their children. Soon families spent time playing together instead of arguing and complaining.

"This town is a different place since Matthew came," said one man.

"Yes," agreed his neighbor. "It is indeed."

It was true. The town had become a happier place. But Matthew was still troubled that no one remembered Christmas.

Late in the year, when the air grew cold and the winds began to blow, Matthew sat in his workshop and began to carve something new.

"What is it?" asked the children. "What are you making now, Matthew?"

"I'm making a crèche," he answered.

As he carved and whittled and carved some more, Matthew told the children a story. He told of the angel who appeared to Mary and how Mary would give birth to a special baby boy. He explained how the angel told Mary to call this baby Jesus because "Jesus" means "the Lord saves."

"This is the angel," Matthew said to the children when he had finished his carving. Sure enough, the wooden figure was a life-size angel.

The children looked at the angel and touched it and admired it.

"What will you carve next, Matthew?" they asked excitedly.

"This will be Mary," said Matthew. He pointed to another large piece of wood leaning against the wall. "And that will be Joseph."

Matthew then told how the angel appeared to Joseph too and how Joseph and Mary traveled together to Bethlehem to be counted for the record books.

And he told them about the first Christmas—about the birth of the Savior, about God the Son.

"Hurry," begged the children then. "Hurry so all will be finished in time for Christmas."

The children told their parents about Matthew's story and about the crèche he was making. Then something wonderful happened. All the people in the town decided to celebrate. For the first time in anyone's memory, they would have Christmas!

Everyone hummed and whistled and sang the carols and hymns Matthew taught while he carved. Mothers stirred up cakes and baked cookies. Fathers said, "Come, everyone, let's go to the woods and cut a Christmas tree." Children busily made colored paper chains and foil stars to hang on their trees.

The people of the town wrapped marvelous Christmas presents to give to others. They decorated their houses and streets with bows and lights. They greeted people they met with smiles and warm words.

Everyone was happy because Christmas was coming.

About a week before Christmas, as the children watched Matthew continue to carve the figures for the crèche, one small boy had an idea.

"My dad knows how to carve. He might like to help."

"Mine does too," chimed in another child.

"And," said a third, "my mom knows how to paint. I'm sure she would like to help."

Matthew smiled a smile so big
that the wrinkles on his face almost hid
his eyes. "Everyone may help," he said
to the children.

Every night after that, mothers
and fathers and children gathered in
Matthew's workshop and carved and
painted and listened to him tell the story
of Christmas. No matter how crowded it
got, no matter how noisy, the families
of the town listened to Matthew talk of
Mary and Joseph, of the angels and the
shepherds, and of the birth of a special
baby on a special night.

At week's end, there were statues of Joseph and Mary, the angel, the shepherds, a donkey, some sheep, and a cow.

"Next Christmas, we will fix up the church and put our crèche in front of it," said a man as he carved the last bit of the last sheep's hoof. "But this year, where will we set our crèche?"

"Let's put it in the city park," a little boy suggested. "Then we can all gather on Christmas Eve to pray and sing."

Everyone agreed.

"But we still have the baby Jesus to carve," said a little girl. "And tomorrow is Christmas Eve."

Matthew smiled. "Baby Jesus will be there by Christmas," he promised.

Long after the people had gone to their homes for the night, Matthew worked to put the finishing touches on the statues.

Then, very early the next morning before anyone noticed, Matthew quietly left the town. All day long people wondered about him and looked for him. "Perhaps he was called away or had an errand to do," the people told one another. "But surely he will come back tonight and bring the baby for the manger."

The whole town was astir. Parents and children were busy cleaning the park, making it into a stable with fresh, sweet hay, and setting the figures there. Before they knew it, evening had come—but Matthew was not to be found.

Time passed. Seven o'clock. No Matthew.

Eight o'clock. No Matthew.

Nine o'clock. And still no Matthew!

"How can we take our children to say a prayer at the crèche when there is no baby Jesus?" asked one mother.

"Don't worry," said another. "I have an idea."
She whispered something in her husband's ear and he exclaimed, "Yes! I will tell the people that the crèche is ready."
Off he went.

When everyone gathered at the crèche late that night, a light was shining all around and the air smelled of fresh hay. And there, in the manger, was a baby lying peacefully under a soft, warm blanket.

"Someone has laid a real baby in the manger!" cried a child.

"That is what Matthew was teaching us," said the father of the baby. "On the first Christmas, God came to earth as a *real live baby*. Remember the Bible verse Matthew told us, 'The Word became flesh and dwelt among us'?"

A murmur arose among the people. "We remember now," they said. "Immanuel, God is with us! It *is* a holy night."

The people of the town understood then.

It was their first Christmas.

But it wasn't their last.

The angel said to them,

"Fear not, for behold, I bring you good news of great joy
that will be for all people. For unto you is born this day
in the city of David a Savior, who is Christ the Lord."

Luke 2:10–11